Bungalo Books
presents

MELODY MOONER

Stayed Up
All Night

Written by Frank B. Edwards
Illustrated by John Bianchi

"It's 7:00. Time for bed,"
called Mortimer Mooner.

"I'm not going to bed," said Melody
Mooner." I'm going to play with my
blaster blocks. All night long!"

"It's 8:00. Time for bed,"
called Mother Mooner.

"I'm not going to bed," said Melody
Mooner. "I'm going to watch
television. All night long!"

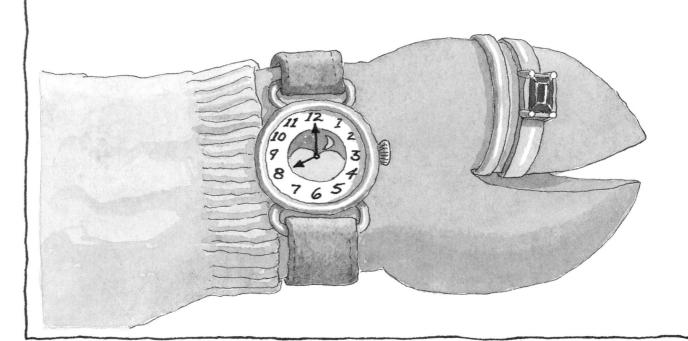

"It's 9:00. Time for bed,"
called Father Mooner.

"I'm not going to bed," said Melody
Mooner. "I'm going to bake cookies.
All night long!"

"It's10:00. Time for bed,"
called Grandmother Mooner.

"I'm not going to bed," said Melody
Mooner." I'm going to play flashlight
tag. All night long!"

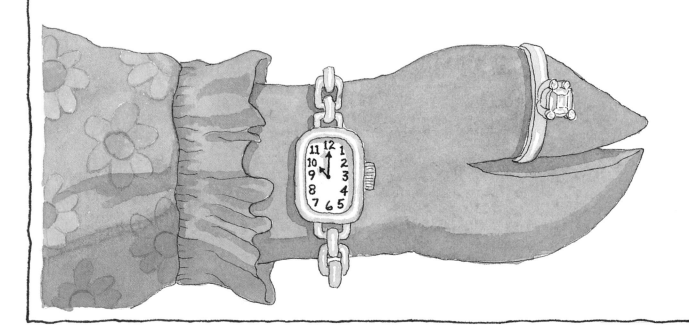

"It's 11:00. Time for bed,"
called Grandfather Mooner.

"I'm not going to bed," said Melody
Mooner. "I'm going to ride my tricycle.
All night long!"

"It's 12:00. We're all going to bed,"
called the Mooners.

"I'm not going to bed," said Melody
Mooner. "I'm going to count the stars.
All night long!"

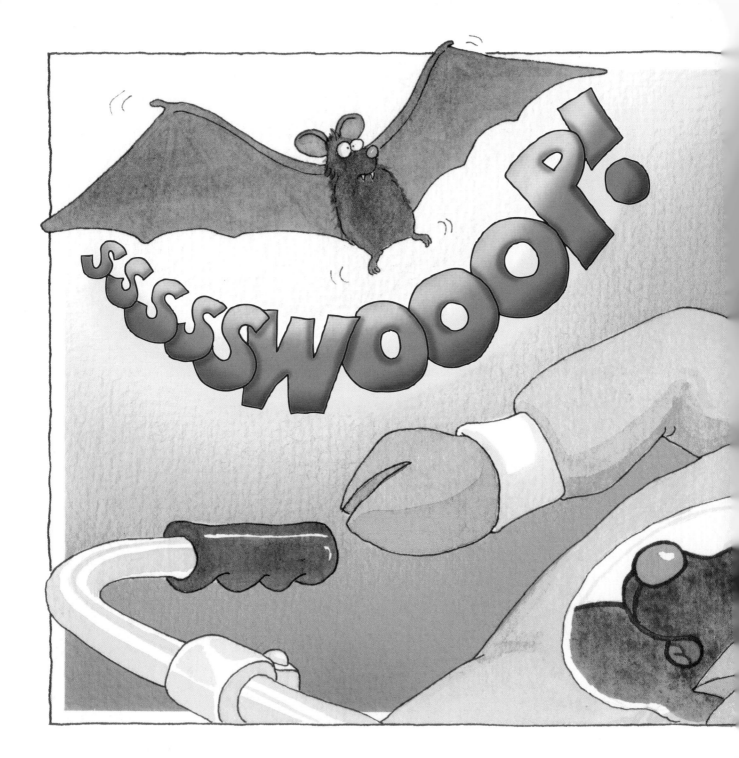

"I think it's time for me to go to bed now," called Melody Mooner.
"And I'm going to sleep.
All night long..."

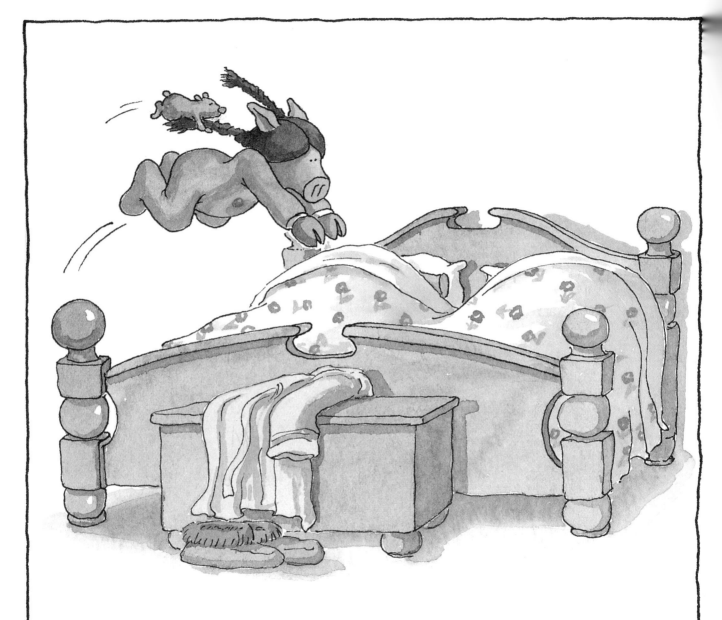

"...with my mom and dad."